W9-AQW-134

MARVEL STUDIOS

SHANG-CHI
AND THE LEGEND OF THE TEN RINGS

WHO GUARDS MY SLEEP?

WRITTEN BY MARIE CHOW   ILLUSTRATED BY SIJA HONG

JESSAMINE COUNTY PUBLIC LIBRARY
600 South Main Street
Nicholasville, KY 40356
(859)885-3523

Shang-Chi,
Xialing,
it's time for
a bedtime
story.

Tonight,
I'll tell you
about the
guardians
of Ta Lo.

Ta Lo? We haven't heard stories about your home village in a long time.
Can you bring us there?

We can
visit Ta Lo
in our
imaginations.

After all,
only Ta Lo's
guardians
are capable
of watching
over my most
precious
treasures.

These are
the Guardian
Lions, or
Shíshī.
石狮

Playful
but loyal,
Guardian Lions
protect each
other and their
loved ones.

Yes. Xialing is cute and clever....

She reminds me of the Nine-Tailed Fox, the Jiu Wěi Hú. 九尾狐

The Nine-Tailed Fox will find special treats from all over the world for you, and just like Xialing, will protect you with her strength and intelligence.

麒麟

The Qílín is
quite unique.

The Qílín
has fish scales
to swim . . .

and feathers
to fly . . .

yet it's
so gentle
it walks in
the clouds
just to protect
the grass.

But like the
two of you,
it is both kind
and powerful.

If it's flight
you want,
then a Phoenix
is the guardian
for you.

凤凰

The Fènghuáng
has beautiful
feathers, and is
known for
its loyalty and
compassion.

A wonderful
choice for my
bold and brave
little one.

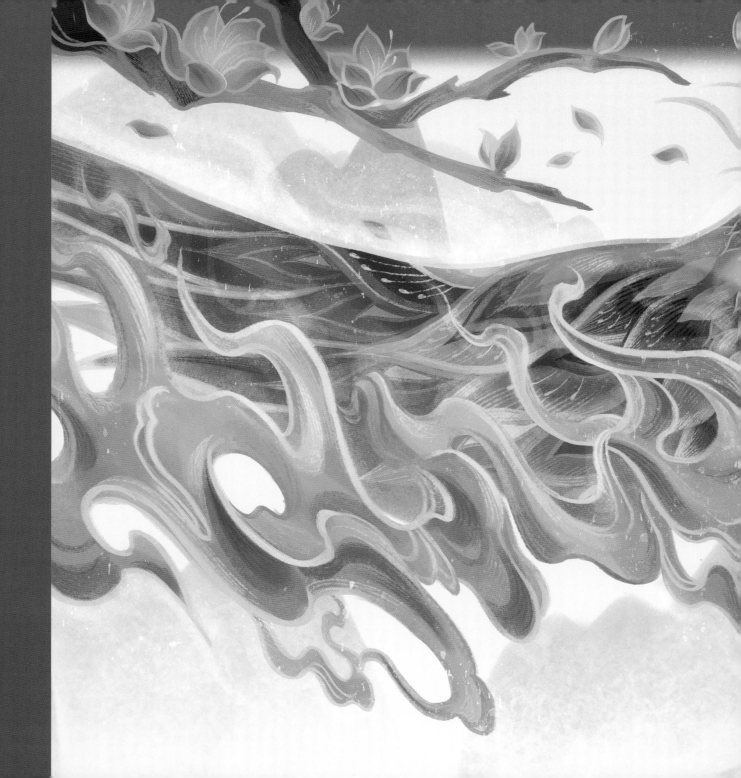

One day,
you may
find yourself
sharing your
knowledge
with others,
like this
carrier of
the scrolls.

And best
of all . . .
the Phoenix
is bathed
in fire and
light to keep
you warm and
safe through
the night.

That is
Morris.

Morris is
a bit more
difficult
to describe
than our
other
guardians.

His actions
will often
surprise
you, but
trust that
Morris is
always on
your side.

This one looks like a Dragon.
Perhaps that is the guardian most like me?

Yes, my Shang-Chi.

Dragons, or Lóng . . .

龙

. . . are very powerful. Dragons won't protect just anything or anyone, but there are no limits to what they will do for their loved ones.

I believe
you'll have
a different
path from
that, my love.

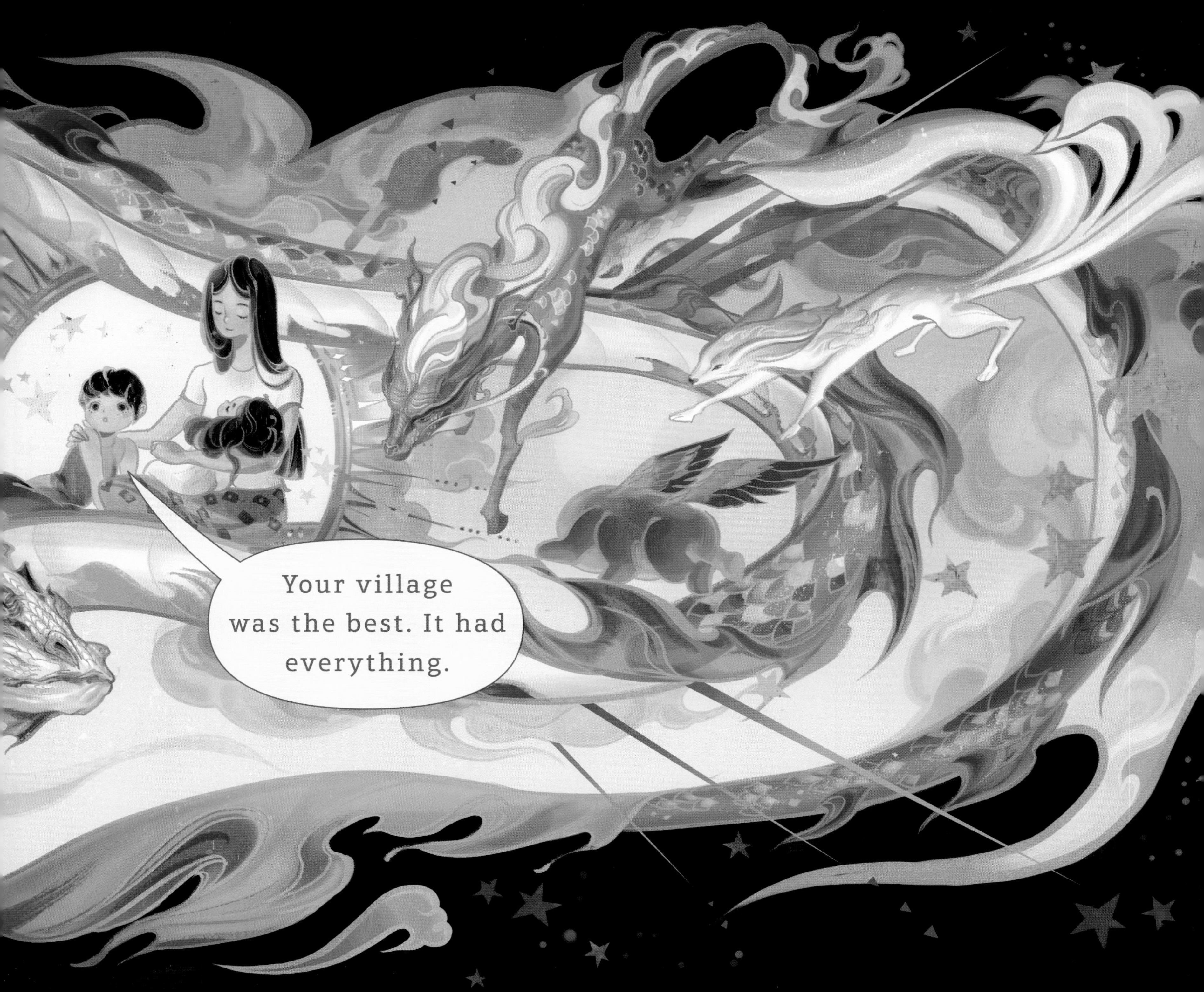
Your village was the best. It had everything.

Not quite . . .
Not quite.

MARVEL

© 2021 MARVEL. All rights reserved. Published by Marvel Press, an imprint of Buena Vista Books, Inc. No part of this book may be reproduced or transmitted in any form or by any means, electronic or mechanical, including photocopying, recording, or by any information storage and retrieval system, without written permission from the publisher. For information address Marvel Press, 77 West 66th Street, New York, New York 10023.

Printed in the United States of America

First Edition, September 2021   10 9 8 7 6 5 4 3 2 1

ISBN: 978-1-368-06996-0

FAC-034274-21204

Library of Congress Control Number: 2021933877

Reinforced binding